I MET A POLAR BEAR

STORY BY SELMA AND PAULINE BOYD
PICTURES BY PATIENCE BREWSTER

Lothrop, Lee & Shepard Books **New York**

Library of Congress Cataloging in Publication Data
Boyd, Selma. I met a polar bear. Summary: A child's tardiness is easily
explained to his teacher: a polar bear, earthworm, ant, and pony all
needed his help. [1. Tardiness—Fiction] I. Boyd, Pauline. II. Brewster,
Patience, ill. III. Title.   PZ7.B693Iap   1983   [E]   ·82-10103
ISBN 0-688-01881-5   ISBN 0-688-01885-8 (lib. bdg.)

For David and Devin—S.B. and P.B.

This one is for you,
Hermie, squirmy, wormy
Holland Chauncey Gregg IV—P.B.

I pushed the big door open and hurried down the empty hall to my room.

When I walked in, everyone stared at me.

"Late again?" my teacher said.

"I met a polar bear," I explained, out of breath.

"A polar bear!" he cried.

"This is what happened," I said patiently.

On my way to school, I met a polar bear. He was standing in the street, helping the school crossing guard.

"Wait a minute!" he said, grabbing my arm and leading me across the street.

"What do you want?" I asked.

"Will you take me to the zoo?" he begged. "It's too hot here."

I put my arm around his soft, furry middle. "Come with me."

I found a bus stop, dug into my pocket, and pulled out a coin.

Watch Your Step

50¢ over 12
25¢ under 12
PAY
HERE
over 65
polar bears
free

A bus marked ZOO stopped. "Get on," I told him.

"I have no money," he answered.

I said, "Polar bears ride free."

The bus was crowded. I took the last seat, and he plopped himself down on my lap. Have you ever held a polar bear?

We got out at the zoo. He leaned against a block of
ice and waved, and I waved back.

Then I skipped down the street so I would get to
school on time.

But my boot came untied. When I bent down
to tie it, I saw a fat earthworm.

He slithered away from the curb and cried, "Help! I'm lost!"

"Where do you live?" I asked.

"In a garden!" he snapped. "Don't you know anything?"

"Three and three are six," I said. "I before e, except after c."

He inched his way closer to me. "I don't like show-offs," he said. "Just get me to a garden. I have work to do. Hurry, before someone puts me on a fishhook!"

I asked him what line of work he was in.

"I get gardens ready for plants," he said. "I dig in dirt."

"I do that, too, sometimes," I told him.

I felt sorry for that little old earthworm, so I stuck him
in my pocket. He went in upside down. "Help!" he cried.
"I'm smothering!"

"Sorry," I said, turning him over. "I'm just trying to help." When we came to a flower box I asked, "What do you think?"

"Put me down," he said. "I'll start digging in these geraniums."

I said goodbye and started on to school.

I stopped at the corner for just a minute to look in the bakery window.

A man came out eating a big cinnamon bun. I went closer to sniff the good smell.

"Get off me!" yelled someone. "Move your big feet!"

I looked down and saw an ant staring up.

"I thought I was a goner!" he said. "You almost crushed me!"

"Sorry," I told him. "Are you all right?"

He picked up a crumb that was as big as he was.

"Maybe I can help you," I said. "Where are you taking the crumb?"

"Back to the ant colony," he answered. "The children are hungry."

I put my finger on the sidewalk, and he crawled onto it
with his crumb.

"I could do this by myself," he said. "I can carry my
own weight and more."

"I don't mind helping," I told him. "Where is the ant colony?"

"Under that rosebush," he said, so that's where I put him down.

More ants came scampering over, and one crawled up my leg. I brushed him off and got out fast.

I was kicking a pebble down the street when I noticed the steeple clock. It said five minutes to nine.

"Can you turn the big hand back?" I asked. "I need a bit more time."

Quick as a flash, the big hand went back five minutes.
"That's not enough," I said. "I need more."

"Maybe I can help you," said a voice.

I took a few steps and saw a pony with a rope fastened
around his neck. The rope was wound around a tree.

"How can you help me?" I asked.

"If you will get me untangled from this tree, I will take you to school," he said.

I got the pony loose.

"Get on my back," he said.

I got on, and we galloped off.

When we got here, I got off the pony and came in as fast as I could.

"And that," I said, "is why I'm late."

"I see," said my teacher, but I didn't hear the rest.

For I saw a friendly face peering through the back window.
I waved. He disappeared.

But I was sure we'd meet again soon.